Amuráti
Sci-Fi & Fantasy

(One-Page Shorts)

VOLUME TWO
FIFTY SHORT STORIES

By
Amurá Oñaā

Published by

UNLIMITED LLC
2020

Other books by Amurá Oñaā

The Promise
(Poem)

Amurati
Vol. 1
(50 Short Stories, 300 words or less)

The Seed
(Origin of AI)

Jonathan Hood in Close the Door Behind You

The Haven House
Co-authored with Joe Hunt

Tainted Times
(100 Days of Prose)

ISBN 978-0-578-73335-7
AMURÁTI SCI-FI & FANTASY
(ONE-PAGE SHORTS, VOLUME 2)

Cover Design and Art by Amurá Oñaā

Published by Amurá Unlimited, LLC

www.amuraunlimited.com

For those Ideas
Found in the Silence
between the
Rain Drops

Introduction

In Amuráti Sci-Fi & Fantasy (Volume II), I approach the same idea of writing fifty short stories in the format of an amuráti, a story with three hundred words or less.

Unlike the stories in Volume one, which was a series of whatever story came first. I decided to focus on the theme of sci-fi and fantasy, writing them in the order that they came to me.

I hope you enjoy reading them. Again, as in volume one, the stories are without titles; they have roman numeral numbers for headings. It is up to the reader to provide the title they think best fits the tale.

At the back of this book is a listing showing the story number and its word-count.

Please note, anyone can write an amuráti. See if you can keep your stories 300 words or less.

Enjoy!

I

The landing was picture perfect for the Audubon-6 spacecraft. The only problem — there was no landing pad and no one there to meet the vessel.

The first communique was a definite affirmative. It had to be, for when it came to corporate confirmations, failure to confirm or comply meant termination.

The Audubon-6 eagerly dispatched an emergency transmission to the base tower, but there was no response from the tower.

The ground crew waited patiently; Audubon-6 was late. The last noted position of the ship was just above the landing zone as an unusual cloud formation passed over the landing area.

Corporate Commander Evans of the ground crew was as impatient as he was nervous. He ordered a corporate-tracking flare launched into the clouds above.

"This crazy planet; damn weather patterns! Get that flare launched! ASAP!" he barked.

"Yes, sir! Flare launched."

"Track that flare through that cloud system."

"Tracking, sir!" came the response.

The flare climbed into the heavens, passed through the cloud coverage, and was gone.

The tower crew waited - nothing; checked their monitors, still nothing. After some exhausting minutes went by, everyone grew nervous. The thought of corporate termination fueled their fears.

"Incoming signal! Incoming signal!" blared in Evan's helmet.

About a minute passed when Evans shouted back, "So where is the flare?"

A nervous voice answered him, "Commander Evans? The signal is coming from a solar system a light-year away!"

"What the hell?"

When the captain of the Audubon-6 scanned the landing site, she realized they were not on UGR-4718. She quickly opened the blast-view window to see a corporate flare coming down through the clouds that were beginning to dissipate, revealing a different star pattern. A crew member yelled, catching her attention only to see gigantic, monstrous creatures rushing toward her spacecraft.

II

The incinerating unit was running full blast when it transferred over to a cremation processor. Two hours passed since its operation mode switched over from an incineration processor to a cremation processor.

The androids operating the units had to meet their quota of torsos of 500,000 before the next change processing rotation; in over twenty years, they never missed their allocation.

Class 24G Androids, waste disposal units, worked 24/7 maintaining the sensitive job of extracting specific minerals from both incinerated and cremated residue.

Recently deployed, Android 87, of the Southern District, was loading torsos onto the conveyor belt. It recognized the body of eleven-year-old Andrew Simmons, the boy it cared for when it was a caretaker model.

The shape of the child startled him; it gave an unexpected glitch to his system, considering the legal termination-age for most humans was fifty cycles. What caused its demise? It paused the conveyor belt and noticed the possible causes.

The android found itself running past data of embedded memories of the child; memories supposedly purged during its last maintenance fitting. There was a conflict with previous data and current programming.

The sensation emoted an unexpected system's failure. It tried to reach the torso, falling into the conveyor belt, and stopping the processor, which lead to an explosion as it held the child tenderly in its arms.

Its malfunction destroyed the plant, upending the extraction of minerals in the Southern District, slowly leading to a system-wide failure across the planet.

III

The game was simple enough to play, as the college boys finished their drinking binge at Timothy's Bar and Grill. The five of them had agreed to play "Stalk-Her." A game where each would pick a woman sitting in the establishment and follow her for at least two hours once she got up to leave.

They hoped that one of the selected women would go home where they could get snapshots of the woman undressing. They would email their pics back to Raymond's computer. The player with the best outrageous photos would win.

They downed their last drinks and quickly followed their targets when they left the bar.

Elliot's target was a beautiful red-headed woman who looked at him intensely while sitting on a barstool. Before leaving, she toasted him as if inviting him to follow her.

Elliot giggled as the other guys joked about it and urged him to go after her; she looked like she desired him.

When she left, she gave him an alluring look before going out the door.

Elliot followed the woman through the streets in the wee hours of the morning, and after an hour of taking snapshots, she finally turned and blew him a kiss before entering a dark alleyway. He took a picture and started to get excited as to what she could have meant by the kiss, putting his phone on video, sending the live feed to Raymond.

Upon turning the corner, a ravenous, female werewolf awaited him and viciously tore him to shreds

Raymond finally got home and checked his email. When he got to Elliot's, all he heard from the live feed were screams that ended with a woman's voice saying, "I can smell your scent on your friend!"

Next, he heard a vicious growl as his door opened.

IV

The musicians gathered for another rehearsal. Those attending agreed at their last rehearsal that if their keyboard player missed any more rehearsals, they would fire him. They had had enough.

Two of them sat at their station while the other two paced the studio shaking their heads in dismay.

"I told you! Didn't I tell you? Uh? His ass never shows up on time! This is the sixth time he hasn't shown. I'm tired, to hell with this!" Stan grabs his instrument and starts packing.

Just then, Ryan comes through the door, sweating profusely and looking exhausted in a half-crazed sort of way.

"Where the hell have you been?" Stan barked.

"You guys, you aren't going to believe this," Ryan said, frantically unveiling them a never-before-seen instrument.

"Is that why you never show up?" asked Stan, packed and ready to leave, but looking curiously at the instrument that Ryan held.

"Somehow, this instrument I built can open a portal in time and allow me to walk through. It's all in a vibrational harmonic and this crystal."

"Right, Stan laughed sarcastically and pushed his gear out the door, slamming it behind him.

Ryan looked back at the remaining band members, "You guys always said our music was way ahead of our time!"

They give him a curious look as he goes about setting up the wiring.

Plucking a chord on the instrument, it puts out a strange eerie hum.

A nurse at Mount Haven Residential Facility made 82-year-old Stan Leonus comfortable in his chair, adjusting his monitor when he heard, ". . . today's new sound in music comes from the band 'Time Ahead!'" The music sounds vaguely familiar. He leans forward, squinting, only to see Ryan and his bandmates, young as on the day he left.

V

Leonard became fixated at the screen displaying photos and writings of his great, great grandfather, famed astronaut William Sotheby. His ancestor's memoirs depicted a yearning for the day when humans would leave their homeworld and traverse the stars. It was a sincere desire that brought tears to Leonard's eyes.

I suppose you'd be proud of me, Papa Bill, I made it, thought Leonard. He sat in his cabin, closing the file, and swiping aside the digital screen that displayed a time long since gone.

He rotated in the chair in his room aboard the famed battle cruiser, Black Hammer, a space vessel of tremendous fighting power.

The yellow cabin lights flashed repeatedly. They were coming out of hyperdrive and entering enemy space.

He locked down his essentials and strapped on his armament.

An alarm soon followed the flashing lights; the ship was under fire.

So soon, thought Leonard as he opened his door to join the troops scrambling down the corridors.

"How did they know we were coming?" he heard some asked.

"It's a damn trap!" came a response.

An explosion on the starboard side left Leonard and others on another final destination. He laid there as the blur of other soldiers ran over his body toward a battle raging amongst the stars appeared through a gaping hole.

As his body began shutting down, Leonard could see Papa Bill's face. Tears came to Leonard's eyes as he said his last words to his ancestor, "Yeah, we made it alright."

VI

The men at the space station were dead. They launched an emergency beacon in a desperate attempt for help; they received none — the chance for rescue ended with the last man's breath.

Evelyn thought she would be tired after moving the 84 corpses to the cargo bay, but she wasn't. She sat at the controls waiting for a response. Two days had already passed. Evelyn looked at the panel and screens in front of her. She recalled some of the conversations and sexual encounters with individual members of the crew.

Evelyn asked herself as she walked the vacant corridors, "Shouldn't I be worried?" Only she wasn't.

She searched for an answer as to why she only survived, and why was she the only female at the station? She investigated the data log for the date of her arrival at the station. There was none, not even a station personal listing of her station or reason for her being on board.

Her inquiry led her back to the station's initial construction, still nothing. She wandered the halls, trying to figure out what to do or who to contact. She even searched for files about her role on the ship's manifest.

She came across a partially deleted file. It took her days to get past the encryption coding.

She learned that she was an android, built to service the sexual needs of a male-dominated culture. She discovered her creator was a woman who had been sexually abused by men. Evelyn purposely held a design "flaw" command: Gradually draw out the lifeforce from all male-sexual encounters, of men with her or men with other men on any part of the station.

Her creator hated men, designing her model to kill them via their lust.

Reading the access file triggered her self-destruct protocol.

VII

The ambassador listened to the rantings of the President on her monitor, "Who do these savages think they are? We should've wiped them out when we first came over decades ago! We civilized them with our religion, cured them of their diseases, and now they're attacking us?"

Diseases you brought them. Thought the ambassador.

There was some commotion behind the President. She turned, and her monitor when blank.

The ambassador waited for a call from her government, ordering an evacuation of the embassy. She was nervous, wondering if they were supposed to stay and wait it out, only to hope for the best.

The incoming reports on the news channels were scanty at best. All reports indicated a civil upheaval to the south of the capital. The tribal warriors from the jungle region were suddenly equipped with far-superior weaponry and were overtaking the nation's military might.

The capital was now under siege and falling rapidly.

The ambassador's communications went down. She heard frantic screaming down the halls of the embassy. Knocks rattled her door. Shaken like a child, she searched the room for a hiding place.

Finally, she composed herself, looked at her anxious security officer, and walked over to the door opening it.

When she opened the door, a stern-face warrior, in full regalia, stood staring back at her.

A shaman walked up from behind him, smiling but looking at her deep in her eyes, motioning to her, "You see, when we pray, our gods come!"

At that moment, a massive, powerful-looking alien in advanced armor that mirrored the tribal warrior outfit, only far more sophisticated, appeared.

The ambassador and her security guard froze.

The shaman nodded his head to her, "You may go, but tell your kind, we will be coming to teach you a lesson about inferiority!"

VIII

Markus, a knight, set out to slay the great dragon, Organus. However, he found the beast in a distant woodland dead from old age. Markus searched the area, and there was no one in sight.

He did what any knight desiring glory and fame; he pulled out his sword and hacked away until he severed the head. He then took it into the city to claim his reward.

The kingdom rained praise down upon him. They knighted him, "Sir Markus the Great, slayer of Organus." They crowned him King and carried him off to the castle where a great feast awaited him. The cardinal blessed him, and the dukes offered him fair maidens to lay with him.

The honor and recognition given him were more than he had ever hoped. He slept like a king, on a golden bed of silk, extraordinarily drunk and sexually exhausted.

Upon waking, he saw another lovely young maiden pouring wine into a goblet. He smiled, wanting more wine, and wanting her. He accepted the cup, drinking his fill, then tossing it aside as he lunged for her. She stepped back out of reach; suddenly, something yanked him back. Marcus fell on the stone floor and noticed a golden lace tied to his ankle.

The maiden handed him a sealed letter, which read:

Hail Great Sir Markus, Ruler of Kardonia, your reputation as a dragon slayer will keep those kingdoms, which war against us, at bay. This magic lace will forever keep you here.

Oh, King, the knowledge of your presence in our high tower will keep us safe. We are forever in your debt. Long live the King!

Know that you can never leave! By order of the Kardonian Council

IX

When they came to meet the village shaman, they exchanged gifts and offered stories. The captain and his lieutenant parleyed with chieftains. At the same time, in the dense forest region, troops belonging to the landing party searched for the precious raw materials scanners had picked up in orbit.

"Our world is far off, far among the stars," Captain Wainwright explained to the shaman, pointing to the heavens. Knowing full well, they could take whatever Wainwright wanted by sheer use of force; he needed no permission concerning these "savages." He followed protocol and asked, "We would like your permission to explore your planet."

Just then, the captain received an urgent call saying that eight members of the eastern search team had vanished, as though the Earth simply swallowed them where they were standing.

Upon hearing the report over the captain's cam, the shaman touched his arm. "I'm sorry to hear such news, but on this planet, you must be careful it's known to eat its inhabitants for sustenance. After all, it is a living creature."

"Are you crazy? That's impossible!" the captain shouted.

"Why? Doesn't your planet eat its own, taking their lifeforce?"

"No!"

"Because you don't know it does, doesn't mean it's not feeding."

"There's no sense in what you're saying."

"Why? Your urge for wars and destruction, your disasters, quakes, volcanoes, storms, and so on, all comes from your planet's bidding: its need to feed. She gives life to feed on the living, prolonging her existence. The mantra of all living planets."

The captain ordered all troops back to their ships. He radioed Earth as to what transpired, only find to hear that a typhoon passed over the station, killing thousands, cutting short his signal, leaving him to look at the planet below him in a new light.

X

The monsters waited outside in the field, knowing they held an advantage. Some would sleep while others stood watch, prowling the perimeter to block off any escape routes.

The event wasn't the first time "visitors" landed on their planet with intentions of dominating their species through superior force. Invaders always assumed they could overthrow their world because the "monsters" living here were ignorant savages.

The "Ausarians," an unknown species, had given up space travel millennia ago for a more peaceful existence, a humbler form of life. There was no need to control their portion of the galaxy as their ancestors had done. They had "found" themselves; their strength was in each other.

Other beings who came across them always viewed them as monsters. Once seeing their form, size, and hearing their roars, it was what they assumed, never knowing that one growl held a thousand bits of information.

The invaders trained their weapons, thinking they would escape with little to no effort. When they stepped out from undercover as their ships entered the atmosphere, the "monsters" gathered and roared. The roar turned into a song that produced such a resonance, the atoms of all things alien to their world began to solidify, crystalizing into stone.

The sound radiated far off into their stratosphere. Planetary vessels who heard rumors about that strange world were wise enough to leave it alone, referring to it as the planet Medusa.

XI

The alarm went off on the mothership, catching the crew at the helm off guard. They didn't expect the sensor to go off for at least another four centuries.

"The humanoids unexpectedly discovered a path to a chamber in the temple on the southern part of the northern hemisphere."

The commander anxiously looked at his captain, "We can't allow them to find what we left there. They're not supposed to discover it for another four hundred years, as a species, they're not ready for that kind of knowledge!"

"Transport the items back to our ship!" the captain shouted.

"That would take longer than we would need."

"A distraction will be needed to be set up. Inform some of our ocean bases to make some flybys in the area of the temple and populated cities."

News reports on Mexican radio and television stations broadcast the discovery. "Archeologists report the discovery of an unearthed temple in the southern region. There's a hidden antechamber. They expect it to hold many secrets and answers to questions asked over the last few centuries."

"This just in, there are new reports of sightings of UFOs over major cities. There's quite an alarming number of them circling about, raising tension in the area. The Armed Forces are on high alert."

"As a follow up to the news story we just shared earlier. The archeological find, to the surprise of researchers, tremors in the southern part of the country have caused the temple in question to collapse, leaving them clueless as to the cause. It may take many decades, if not centuries, to remove the debris safely without causing further damage. Stay tuned."

XII

Dr. Brandon Curtis wasn't one for writing down formulas. He never kept records; he simply retained all his procedures with his photographic memory, another aspect of his many gifts.

His ego slowly found a seat at the throne of his genius, leaving him to deny access to his work and findings by other "pretenders in the field of science."

Finally, one day, things came together in his lab. He had completed the "elixir of life" that had escaped researchers for millennia.

He opened the door to his sedated human subject, a volunteer prisoner, convicted of corporate espionage resulting in the death of several investors. Dr. Curtis didn't know his name; he didn't want to know. He needed to proceed with the experiment before his colleagues arrived. If he failed, they would denounce his efforts; if he succeeded, they would want to share in his discovery.

Brandon wheeled a table over to the convict and injected the formula into his subject. Violent contortions followed, similar to reactions in his earlier failed tests, only this time by the time they subsided, the patient was visibly ten years younger.

He had to unstrap the patient for further tests. The process had awakened the subject who, upon seeing himself in the overhead mirror, realized the change.

He recognized profit when he saw it. He jumped off the examination bed and grabbed the doctor, hoping to steal the formula; they struggled with him striking Dr. Curtis, killing him.

The formula shattered as the doctor fell, knocking it to the floor. The convict searched for documents, only to finally get subdued by incoming colleagues who called security. He was sentenced to life, to die in prison. Unfortunately, there was a problem; the formula kept renewing his genes, making him two days younger for every passing day.

XIII

The bats came out in the tens of thousands, blanketing the early evening sky liken to a sheet of darkness drawn across the heavens.

The vampire watched from his lair as he smiled at his cousins. He lifted his wings to join them in flight.

He heard rumors of a young, beautiful woman tending to her chores in a village west of his location.

He was sure he could turn her. She would be the first wife of his pride. He could hear the drums from her village beating through the night sky as he flew above.

He landed not far from her and assumed the form of a handsome and wealthy black merchant.

She stood up from her chores, looking in his direction, admiring this stranger as he knew she would.

Before he could ask for a drink, she offered him some. He spoke in a voice she found soothing to the ear and enticing to the heart. He drew her into his arms. Without hesitation, he caressed her, sinking his fangs into her neck. She moaned with excited passion.

He released her to admire his effect on her.

She swooned back, taking her fingers and gently collecting the blood running down her neck. Tasting it, she opened her eyes slowly, smiling at this vampire. She let out a laugh as she turned into a sharp-fanged leopard of the night and devoured him as he screamed in agony. She might have been the first of his pride, but he was just another meal.

The virus, traveling across the cosmos, would attach itself to whatever gravitational pull that would influence it, provided there was a consumable life force available. The expanse of the "viral system" would often cross several solar systems.

It was slow-moving, but ever on the move. In some quadrants of the galaxy, the virus was well known. Civilizations had given it a host of names in various tongues: Death's Harbinger, the Cycle of the Forgotten, along with other foreboding titles.

There was an intelligence to it. It would infect lifeforms causing them to release their life force on which the virus would feed, breed, and multiply — using the remains of the energy to lift off a consumed planet and rejoin the continuum.

In the 24th century, a warning of a virus approaching the Earth was given earlier in the mid-22nd century. Over one hundred fifty years had gone by offering the species of the Earth to prepare or relocate in another habitable solar system.

Humanity was too busy dismissing the myths surrounding the virus. They never realized that by the time the virus reached the outer colonies, it would be too late for their home planet to respond. The most they could do was send a beacon-satellite to warn other solar systems.

The alien species who found the satellite containing the plaque and data stream had finally interpreted the encrypted message of the demise of a planet called Earth. They turned over their findings to the authorities on their world so that they could prepare.

XV

Clearing out the landing zone was more readily accessible than initially anticipated. Was it because the hostiles were simply waiting to attack when our guard was down? Were they hurt so severely, they couldn't respond and needed time to lick their wounds as our commander had claimed?

I waited at my post, watching others from our unit, clearing away the debris from crashed ships.

Hostiles? I never did like that term. Maybe because we were the hostiles, considering it was our species that invaded their planet, this God-forsaken rock locked in orbit around a red giant.

I've been on enough missions to know how this will appear in our records. A victory will claim that our brave, fearless troops conquered them as backward savages deserving annihilation. A loss will note them as unconquerable beasts attacking in superior numbers, and that we were fortunate enough to have survived the encounter. In either case, they would be the monsters in this exchange.

My squad leader often says that I overthink things. Not to worry, I understand my role as a pawn, a gear in the war machine, and I'll do my part as always. Somedays, however, I wonder what the records of the species on this planet will say about us.

One can only imagine.

XVI

He waited in the quiet shadows, those hidden spaces in the realm no one gave attention. Humans who evolved the "single story" and accepted this illusion commonly and ignorantly called reality, were most vulnerable.

It wouldn't take long; it never was. The creature was human once, had grown quite accustomed to the habits, the flaws, and tendencies of men and women. Only those humans gifted with sight could spot them from time to time. Those people referred to his kind as the greys.

Greys like him would reside in the shadows waiting to strike the "sleepers," the name given to those humans blindly going about their daily lives.

He knew that every so often, there would be a "dreamer" among the sleepers. One willing and ready to sprout out their ideas and elevate themselves in the eyes of others, continually feeding the appetite of their egos, enriching themselves, and enhancing their taste, but never achieving anything.

Dreamers were the most delicious of the human targets. Rather than showing the wisdom to sit on their dreams and nurture them until they hatched accurately. They put out the vibrant energy of a new idea and would offer him a grand feast.

No, he didn't mind the waiting; his favorites were ripe. They glistened with anticipation in the darkness. There was always the chance to occupy the body of a particular sleeper. Those who were as hungry as him, willing to eat the dreams and ideas of the vibrant ones. He could have such a swell time hiding in their shadows. Here comes one now.

XVII

Ansari, the Prince, left the city and entered the woods to contemplate the impending death of his father, the King.

He stopped at his favorite spot by the lake and proceeded to take a drink. When he bent over to take a drink, the face of a young maiden appeared, startling him. She shook her head at him, causing him to jump back.

A massive tree branch fell, just where he stood a moment ago. He would have died had he drank from that spot.

He cautiously edged back to the lake when the ripples subsided, but she was no longer there.

When he returned, he met by his uncle and other elders, an uncle who wanted the throne. They extended to him a goblet of wine, likened to the ones they all carried. His father, the King, was dead. They needed to take a ceremonial drink to honor his passing.

Ansari, saddened by the news, raised his cup to drink only to see the maiden's face reflecting in the gourd, shaking her head. He fane as if to fall.

His uncle put out his arms catch grab him, placing his gourd and his nephew's gourd on the ground.

Ansari collected himself and rose, taking his uncle's cup. All bowed and drank. His uncle smiled at his nephew, only to fall to his knees, convulsing. He dropped dead. Startled by the event, three elders pointed fingers at each other, accusing one another of the misdeed.

The new King Ansari handed them into custody for treason against the crown.

During his reigned, he learned of the tale of a young princess who ages ago promised to protect her people from the world beyond. Ansari believed it was she who kept her promise.

He honored her with libations.

XVIII

Sir Reginald had heard about Lady Marianna's beauty and the wealth contained in her dowry. Her charm was pretty much average among the elite, nothing to get excited about, but hear-tell, her wealth was enough to save his failing kingdom, threefold.

"Her appearance, I can learn to live with, but her wealth must be mine," he loudly declared to his squire, who saddled his steed.

"So good, sir, there is no love in your heart for the fair maiden?" the young man asked, kneeling so his master could step on him and mount his horse.

Sir Reginald gave him a glance saying, "Well, if you have to ask . . . Never mind. How do I look? Do I have enough jewels on me?"

The squire stepped back to take in his lord's appearance. "You have more than enough, good sir."

Before the lad could finish his words, the knight was off to Marianna's palace.

When he arrived, there were many mounts from other suitors.

"Other suitors! How dare they!" he said to himself.

He was met at the palace gate by a guard who asked, "And you are?"

"Sir Reginald of South Netherland," he boldly stated.

"Would you see Lady Marianna or her dowry, sir?" the guard asked.

Reginald thought for a second, raised an eyebrow, and smiled, "Her dowry, of course."

The guard took him to the dowry chamber and opened an extravagant chest.

Reginald so astounded by the amount of wealth within, he found he couldn't move. Before he could say a word, he screamed in pain as the trunk viciously sucked him, his armor, and his jewels into the chest. Afterward, it slammed shut.

The guard quietly turned around and returned to his post, sending word to inform Lardy Marianna that her wealth had grown considerably.

XIX

Arthur had lived longer than most. Many of his memories were now lost or forgotten due to Alzheimer's, but of those few remaining, his love of music, and those who cared for him, he seemed to know they must have been good memories.

As his condition was detected early in his life, he arranged to have his body placed in cryofreeze before his condition worsened to an extreme point. When a cure for Alzheimer's became available, he would be brought back to life and feast on the fondness of a full-life experience.

It was eighty-seven years after being placed in cryofreeze that the medical and scientific communities discovered a cure for the disease as well to extend human life for an extra one hundred years or so.

Under the provisions of his contract, they revived Arthur's body. It was a joyous occasion filled with tears and laughter over events long forgotten as they came into his awareness. Still, Arthur was astounded that no one in the recovery room showed any appreciation for his newfound joy.

Doctors immediately ushered him down the hall to another room where he met the legal magistrate of his province, who looked at Arthur's smiling face and read him the law of the region.

"As a representative of the Federation of the New Order. Arthur McAlister, you have broken the law in expressing an emotion of any kind. Therefore, with the life-extension rules of an estimated ninety-two more years, you will receive as of this date, January 22, 2246, appropriate medication and genetic enhancements that would nullify any feelings of any kind, past, present, or future."

"What the . . ."

And with the verdict administered, doctors calmly initiated the procedure to remove emotions. Arthur would become as one of them, considerably enhanced.

The trail of the Sunanthian murderer, who the bounty hunter was tracking, was cold, virtually frozen.

He set his craft on autopilot as it sped to the last known solar system of his prey. He maneuvered his way through his cramp ship to his tiny quarters and assumed a meditative posture.

The bounty hunter needed to search the system with his mind, spirit, and all available senses. After a time in a deep trance, he quietly rose from his seat with eyes remaining closed, guided his way back to his cockpit.

With eyes still closed, he punched in coordinates, opened his eyes, and then landed his ship in a small, out of the way spaceport on the outskirts of major metropolises

Securing his spacecraft, he walked over to the port cantina, brought a drink, and sat by the door.

Two hours later, a tall, lanky Sunanthian walked in and proceeded to the bar. In the overhead, bar mirror he caught the reflection of the bounty hunter who had been chasing him. He turned quickly and fired his blaster at the bounty hunter, hitting him in the chest, only to see a hole in the seat behind his target.

The real bounty hunter came up from the other side of the bar and placed his blaster to the Sunanthian's head.

"Hands behind you or die!"

"But how?" his captive exclaimed, dropping his weapon and placing his hands behind him. "You were 'a solid,' I shot you!"

"Meditation," the bounty hunter stated, knowing he placed the image of himself in the Sunanthian's mind. As he put the cuffs on him, he added, "You'll have plenty of time to learn about it where you're going, if you can."

XXI

The Season of the Snow Wolves would pass. The very creatures the season was named after waited in the woods alongside the outer edge of the village. Instinctively they knew that when the snow fell hard, it was then that the villagers were on guard the most, protecting their families, especially their children.

The beasts were aware of this, for, at one time, each had been a village child. They came to the town to add one more child to their wolfpack, a ritual done every year.

Harley, the butcher's son, was knocked to the floor a third time by his drunken father. He did his best to defend his mother from his father's assaults, but he was not yet capable of such an act.

The howling snowstorm outside kept other villagers from hearing his mother's screams. She watched her husband drag her son to the door and toss him out into the storm. She couldn't get up to stop him, thinking he would kill Harley.

Harley got up, rearing in pain, he saw two guards and ran to them for help. They laughed at the boy, telling him it was nothing and to go back home.

They left the boy mad and angry. Harley struggled to the edge of the woods screaming, "Take me!"

Two snow-white wolves came biting him in the neck. In an instant, he became one of them, a massive beast. The wolves got what they came for and took off for the woods.

Harley's memory of his mother was still fresh, as a new wolf, camouflaged by the snow, he worked his way back to his house, crashed through the window, and ripped his father's throat out.

His mother screamed but noticed the beast had her son's discolored eyes. He turned to join his pack.

XXII

Evans strapped on his spacesuit, waiting to make his run across the craggy face of an asteroid capable of cutting his suit to shreds with one misstep.

His shipmates eagerly watched his run shown through his helmet cam on the ship's monitor. They placed wagers on his survival, hoping for an exciting misstep that would liven up their mood. Their tour along the asteroid belt was boring, and asteroid runs were a way to give them a form of excitement, even if someone died from it.

Evans was more agile than most, and he was out for a new record, pacing his jumps, timing his leaps, thinking of the money he would make when he got back.

"Look at him," cried one of the crew, "He's a dead man. Two hundred credits, he'll never make it back alive!"

"200, and I'll raise you 50 he does!" came a call from the other end of the ship's bar.

Evans leaped high enough to see an oncoming asteroid heading directly for his ship. His only hope was that his crew would see it through his helmet cam.

They did see it on their monitors, appearing out of nowhere, buy it was too late for them to react. The asteroid hit the ship before it could lift off.

Evans looked back at the explosion and was horrified. His focus gone, Evans landed on a thin layer on the surface, crashing into the asteroid into what appeared to be a control room.

Two creatures appear in front of him, subdued him, and then placed shackles on his hands and feet. They dragged him to what appeared to a room full of other alien lifeforms and locked him in a cage. He realized the asteroid itself was a spacecraft collecting specimens

XXIII

It was time for surgery; the doctors arrived at Milton's bedside carrying The Box. They needed him conscious during an intricate and complicated medical procedure, but local anesthetics would not suffice.

Placing a patient's consciousness in The Box would retain an active connection to the patient wherein the patient could respond through ultra-violet frequencies that doctors would read during the surgical process.

The procedure was somewhat new, but it proved to be effective with patients suffering from similar conditions.

The doctors placed The Box by Milton's head. He could feel his consciousness drawn out, as though it pulled him from one room into another that was dark. He could remember the assurances given to him by the professional staff. They would take his consciousness to a shelter room below, where he would be safe.

Once "fitted," the doctors took his body to the surgical arena.

A massive 8.9 earthquake suddenly hit his hospital's city. Thousands died; many were buried alive.

It's been twenty-three years since that horrific event. Much of the city is still underground, and scientists are very vague about their approach to handling the excavation. By chance, they found the Box containing Milton's consciousness ten years ago but never finding his body. He has lost his sense of time; the only thing he knows is the darkness that still surrounds him.

Unable to discover what procedures could be used to transfer his consciousness elsewhere, and under protests by civil organizations demanding that he be left to die, by destroying the Box, the most they could come up with was to place the Box on display in the Museum of Unnatural Sciences.

XXIV

He searched the ruins, not quite sure what the item was he was seeking. Now and again, he would unfold a worn page, torn from a sacred tome, read the text, replace it in his pocket, and continue exploring the ruins.

Was it a key to a crystal or a crystal to a key? The wizard Magnus felt drained, weak, and exhausted from his task. His pupil had collapsed hours earlier and was resting at their campsite. Magnus would continuously look over his shoulder to guesstimate the position of the setting sun and its relation to the horizon. From his observations, he knew he had to save his world. It was near its end.

He heard a strange chime and rushed toward its direction, knocking over the contents from a tall bookshelf. There, amongst the fallen debris, was a key that resembled the key on the scroll.

Perspiring from excitement, he rushed to take out the page, only to wind up smudging the text with his sweaty hands.

As he turned the key in one hand, a crystal appeared in his other hand, partially igniting the paper, burning a good portion of it.

Magnus had spent so much time scouring the ruins; he never really memorized the mantra on the page. Magnus, now holding crystal and key, placed the gem in the key's setting.

With the sun setting behind him, he mumbled what he thought the chant to be, only to hear a voice say, "Wrong again."

"What name do you choose for your son?" asked the village chieftain.

"Magnus," said the steward holding the babe in his arms.

"Then Magnus it is. May he prove wise enough to save us in our time of need."

XXV

There was no way of knowing that the spaceship traveling through the Norris Nebula would attract strange levels of consciousness to their spacecraft.

Hyper-sleep left the crew and their passengers accessible to souls that were captured by the nebula's unique electromagnetic field. The nebula captured souls transmigrating from one part of the galaxy to another.

It was an unfortunate rarity; still, it happened on occasion across the cosmos. It was a reason why some space-faring species carried mystics or "sensitives" aboard their vessels. They would be fitted with aura filters so that even in hyper-sleep, he or she could detect anomalies, setting off alarms to steering ships away to safety.

Unfortunately for the crew traveling through this region of space, no such knowledge existed.

When the ship reached its planetary destination, it had to be guided into the spaceport using autopilot, for no one aboard the craft spoke any recognizable tongue or language upon waking up from their sleep chambers.

It was as if each person belonged to a different species, all looking the same but sounding completely different. A few even panicked at the sight of their reflections.

Linguists and others with computerized translators arrived, deciphering a few languages belonging to totally different types of beings from across other regions of space from those speaking. Some demanded their return to the planets of the spirits inside them. They did not know where they were or how to find them. Other passengers and crew agreed to relearn the dialects of their base planets to blend in, but memories of their past lives of the souls possessing them would be with them until they died. They would be strangers in a strange land.

The flight went down in space historical travel records as "The Flight of Babylon Lost."

XXVI

The Fairfield Forest grew darker and deeper as the hunters frantically searched for their prey that fearfully raced further and further away from them, seemingly seeking refuge in the dense area.

The attention of the hunters was shattered by loud moans that appeared to emanate from the surrounding trees. A kind of wail that rose from the roots of they passed over, causing birds to flutter skyward.

It sounded more like an offering of questions, causing older trees to respond in kind.

The large-antler deer they were pursuing stopped and looked back at them. It would take the hunters a while to reach him or get a clear shot. The deer rubbed up against an ancient tree to awaken it.

When the tree awoke, the deer spoke, "These are the ones who cut down your seedlings and kill my kind. I brought them to you as promised. Now release my kin."

"We are sorry, but we needed you to bring them to us. Here is your family. Now go, it is time we take some of their kind."

The deer fled with its family, as the trees moved closer and closer together toward the confused hunters. When the deer cleared the area, only the screams of the predators could be heard far behind them.

XXVII

As a child, all he could remember was the constant daily ordeal of painful injections at the base of his skull. His parents never explained the reason behind the procedure. They simply said that they would tell him why when he became an adult.

However, when he was ten, both his parents died in a fatal car accident while returning home from a seminar in Arizona with more medication.

Aaron lived with foster parents who only knew his parents from temple worship but were willing to accept him as their own.

Injections were still a requirement, but he never told them, having hidden the remaining medication. He didn't give a damn, as long as those injections were over and done.

Years later, he awoke on the morning of his eighteenth birthday and noticed lizard-like scales on every exposed area of his body. He jumped out of bed and quickly hid in the bathroom.

In the mirror, he no longer appeared human, but a lizard with a forked-tongue and slanted cat-like eyes.

An implanted tracking device in the nap of his neck became activated, emitting a low hum. He grabbed at his neck with claws that were once his hands.

In a panic, he ran to the window only to see a van pull up, with two men stepping out and ringing his bell. His family answered the door, only to be subjected to knockout gas as the men came up and forced his door open.

Both transformed into lizard men, saying, "You should've continued with your injections. We are aliens from a dying world; now, we'll return you to our base to ensure your abilities to blend in with Earthers."

Aaron struggled with them until they subdued him; they brought him back to the van and drove off to Arizona!

XXVIII

The Stolle had conquered as many advanced worlds as they came across in a large sector of their galaxy.

The only reason why they landed on the backward planet of Khadia was because of its incredible abundance of natural resources.

An untold number of crafts landed on Khadia, and troops poured out in mass toward villages containing several thousand inhabitants.

Stolle troops fired on the villages in an all-out effort to eradicate everyone. Villagers immediately sat down and began resonating a forceful sound, joined in by surrounding creatures, plant life, even the planet added to the harmonics of the note.

The space surrounding the Stolle began to dissipate, and they found themselves not only floating above an unknown world in another part of the galaxy but in another dimension altogether.

Slowly the space around them began to solidify, closing in all around them, sealing them in a crystalline state.

The villagers, animals, and plants awoke as if from a trance and went about their daily activities as if nothing ever happen. The tone from the planet had cleared as well.

There was never any mention of the Stolle as it had been in many previous planetary invasions of Khadia.

A vast menagerie of beings from around the galaxy, who attempted to invade the planet Khadia, now existed, crystallized in an unknown dimension.

XXIX

An online social group that Irene belonged to felt that the Chicago members should finally meet to get to know each other better. Irene wasn't a social person and wasn't as enthusiastic as the other members were when it came to attending such events.

Her online friends insisted that she come; it would be such a great chance to meet as they had promised.

"I don't think any of you would like me," she would text them. "I kind of suck."

"Nonsense" was the general response.

Her friends wouldn't have anything to do with that kind of attitude. They offered a positive, encouraging approach to lift her spirits and boost her confidence. Irene finally relented and consented to join them after feeling the pressure.

Irene wanted to look her best as she prepared to go, putting on one of her favorite outfits.

At the meeting hall, a large group of social friends gathered, listening to the music and exchanging tidbits of conversation.

They all turned to see a redhead come in through the door with the nametag Irene. They lit up with smiles and came over to her with open arms.

From out of the side of Irene's outfit came tentacles that pierced eight of the people closest to her as she viciously began to suck out their bodily fluids.

Screams from a woman near her, "Oh my God, what the...?"

Irene looked up, sending another tentacle through her chest, "I told you I suck!"

XXX

Living in the streets as a bum was not on Adria's bucket list, but here she was, nine years after the fall of the Centarus regime of her world.

A former high valued soldier of the Endicott Era of Free Thought, she had PTSD. She was a pitiful sight, fighting over garbage scrapes with planetary rodents, some extremely venomous.

Adria turned in a fallen soldier's weapon at their surrender. She never surrendered her gun, though; she had come to honor it as if it were a dear, trusted friend.

While spitting out the remnants of someone's discarded meal, her gaze caught sight of a Vanglorian starship slowing hovering toward her and the city she came to call home.

It was their flagship, slowing arriving from her west, to sign a peace accord with the new government.

Adria didn't know anything about why it was there. She had been out of touch with current events since she returned home.

She automatically went into combat mode. She was a specialist at taking down such crafts. With two shells left, Adris scrambled to a deserted rooftop and aimed her weapon at a small opening next to the ship's primary vents. Hidden from sight, she fired the two remaining rounds, and the flagship went down, crashing into the capital city.

For all she knew, for all she cared about, the war would continue.

XXXI

Going through the files was exhausting. Hours had turned into days, leaving little to no chance for much-needed rest.

However, Katrina was an officer on board the Meridian spacecraft, and there had been a murder of a crewman.

She had to investigate the background of every passenger and every crewman on board.

After going over logs of recordings at the time when the event took place and performing meticulous background checks, she was beginning to narrow down possible leads.

There was something suspicious about Lieutenant Martin. She took a guard with her when she went to speak with him in his cabin.

As she walked down the corridor, she kept thinking about a death certificate with his name on it from two cycles ago, hidden in a partially corrupted file. She could only get a poor printout of it, and she figured she'd show it to him and confront him about it.

Katrina bypassed the security codes. Her gun and crewmate's gun ware drawn as a precaution when she entered the lieutenant's cabin.

He acted somewhat startled when he turned and noticed Katrina and the guard. He placed his drink on the table and raised his hands.

"Lieutenant Martin, can you explain this printout?" she said as she approached him.

He suddenly deconstructed into thirty insect-like creatures that swiftly leaped onto the startled Katrine and her guard. The creatures devoured them, and then after a short period of mating and birthing new creatures, they reconstructed Martin, Katrina, and the guard.

They bowed to each other as was their way. The renewed Katrina destroyed the copy of the death certificate. She and the guard calmly walked out of the cabin to consume others and make more of themselves.

XXXII

The disabled crew landed their ship on a planet where they knew no one would come to save them. It was a quarantined planet, and for Sorelians, their only hope was to repair the ship themselves.

They had to land; there was no other choice for their spacecraft was about to blow up in orbit.

Once on the surface, they could make the necessary repairs to the electrical system, but they had little time to do it.

They estimated a certain amount of time. Sadly, the Sorelians were wrong.

Within minutes they were hallucinating and experiencing all kinds of strange images and visions.

Only one crewman, Surenia, seemed immune from the planet's effects. She was able to make the required repairs while avoiding other crewmen. With some difficulty, she got the spacecraft back into orbit.

Once in orbit, her crewmen appear to normalize. Even the captain came over to her and thanked her for her efforts. He could see what was taking place on one aspect but could not control the re-emerging effects of the planet.

Everyone assumed their console position, leaving her to presume they had come back to their senses. She felt a considerable sense of relief.

The captain turned the ship around and headed directly for the planet's surface.

She screamed, "Sir, what are you doing?"

He smiled with the eyes of a maniac, saying, "The planet wants us. We must give our lives. The planet may show us strange images, but her song, oh, her song!" The other crewmen agreed, grabbing hold of Surenia.

They headed straight for the planet's surface and crashed!

XXXIII

For all Mandrake knew, magic was real. It was in its subtleties, and not the theatrical imagery people longed to witness with eyes wide open.

He was aware of its effects; he would perceive them days later or weeks beyond the spoken word.

Mandrake knew the power behind the spoken word, how it could linger, and then reinforced through repetition. He had a group of spells that he would cast daily, and like a scientist of the new age, he would study its effects on people and things, recording his work.

He especially enjoyed the study of crippling incantations. One of his most particular subjects was Linda, a woman from his village who had spurned his affections.

Within two months, he had seen her health consumed by ailments attributed to his incantations. He would smile at the subtlety.

One day the Mandrake was reviewing his notes, he noticed one of his record books missing. It wasn't on the bookshelf in his living quarters or among the books in his leather bag.

After a while, he started developing a bad cough that left him weak as if his chest were about to explode.

As he was leaving his favorite café, he collapsed in the street, coughing up blood. A young woman ran up to him as he was puking up blood, sticking her face violently close to his.

"So, you think you can hurt my sister, Linda, do you? Well, what you can do, I can do tenfold, you bastard. I found this book of yours a month ago!" She held his missing record book in her shaking hand, poking it with her finger, whispering his own spell back to him, finishing with, "Die, won't you!"

She got up and left before a crowd gathered, leaving him dead in the street.

XXXIV

His nation asked him to join the fleet early in his career. All the propaganda he had heard growing up had left his nation's mark on him, and he was well-groomed in his allegiance to the regime.

Now, Ardanius found himself in a shattered part of his ship, high above a race of beings willing to offer clones of themselves over and over to defeat him and his allies. His spacecraft landed to make repairs while continuing the fight on the surface.

His left leg, nearly blown clean off, hurt beyond his wildest dreams. Ardanius did his best to control the bleeding. He laid with his weapon at his side, firing it through the damaged hull of his ship at the clones running across the open field, advancing ever so close to him.

With every shot he took, he realized these creatures looked nothing like the pictures of the enemy his commanders told him he would be meeting in combat.

Like so many recruits before him, they lied. He was just another pawn in a game of chess in another campaign for conquest.

As many creatures as he shot, more seem to come, gaining closer to him.

The alien creatures finally broke into where he laid. They injected him with a syringe, and he began changing into one of them with a new leg. Before his transformation, he realized he was not shooting clones of the enemy, but his troops altered to become the enemy.

He stood and nodded at his alien comrades. He reloaded his weapon. Then joined in the battle to destroy those who had once been his fellow officers and comrades.

XXXV

The villagers refused to listen to the young girl. She had told them so many lies over the years, their trust in her was virtually gone.

She saw a red-eyed creature, with eyes that glowed in the dark, roaming the woods at night while she was bringing food to her parent's cabin.

It seemed to be watching the village square while perched on the ravine near the town.

Many of the people just laughed and mocked her as a silly troublemaker, and that people shouldn't believe her.

She pleaded with them, apologizing for all the times she had lied in the past. Something was coming for them, and whatever it was, it wasn't human.

Most of the people waved her off, dismissing her for a lunatic.

However, an older woman sitting off to the side recalled a sixty-year-old curse brought upon the village ages ago. She had heard it when she was a child.

She collected her things and caught the arm of the young girl as she passed.

"Gather your parents and come to my home tonight. There you will be safe."

The girl was surprised, pulling her arm away. Considering her offer as she walked away.

"Tonight, before the sun sets," the old woman warned her.

The girl came back before the sunset, but she came back alone. Her parents didn't believe her.

The woman told her the story of Rufus, killed, burned alive by townspeople ages ago, and swore to take revenge one day.

She had protected her house with charms over the years, knowing this day would come.

Later that night, as they huddled by the fireplace, they could hear the screams of the townspeople crying out in the night. They could hear the creature, but it could not enter.

The girl never lied again.

The rich lords welcomed the knight who had fought valiantly for their kingdom. He was unknown to them, but according to the war records, he had slaughtered an untold number on the battlefield.

They say he had no name. In truth, he could not speak, only mutter a sort of growl.

Still visibly, they treated him with respect, not wanting to dishonor him in any way. However, when they were amongst themselves, they joked about his human failings.

They asked him to accompany them to a chamber where they discussed the near end of the war and the new campaign against the dragons of the north.

He calmly stood in their midst, nodding his head to some of the strategies they proposed, offering them a look of confidence. They admired his aura of strength.

They agreed upon a plan of attack against the dragons, drinking wine to seal the deal.

That night the young knight walked along the ramparts of the castle. He growled in a high pitch tone into the night sky. When he finished, he went down to the castle gates and quietly unlocked them.

In the morning, when the lords and other soldiers awoke, there were fifty to sixty dragons from the north hovering outside the castle walls.

Their knight stood in the castle courtyard and growled, slowly transforming into a tremendous northern dragon. The other dragons entered, some flying in, others coming through the gate.

It did not take long to wipe out the lords' army and all the inhabitants in the castle.

XXXVII

Adriana meddled in enough magical conjuring to assume she knew enough to bring her husband back from the dead.

She held onto his body for longer than she should have, keeping his death a secret from the townspeople.

She did her best to lessen the odor of his body with fragrances and potpourri. The less the neighbors knew, the better she felt.

It took her somewhat longer than she wanted to gather her concoctions, but finally, she felt she was ready.

On the night of a full moon, she performed the strange and powerful ritual to bring her husband back to life. After two hours of spells, she collapsed on the floor of her cabin, exhausted.

With tired muscles, Adriana came to, startled that all her efforts showed no results. She sadly crumbled into an old wooden chair, disappointed with all her plans and preparations.

Later around midnight, there was a quiet groan; she saw the body of her husband try to raise himself on the table.

She rushed over to his side to help, surprised, but happy at what was taking place. "Peter? Peter, is it you, my love?"

"No," he said. "Peter has moved on; I am Naga, cursed to walk the spirit realm for killing many women and children in my day. I was passing by when I heard your ritual. Behold, I am whole again, thank you," he said, and with that, he grabbed a knife off her counter and stabbed her to death.

The young people heard of a haunted house near the edge of town. Christine, Dan, Oliver, and Joan, they had a nickname for their four-some – The Musketeers.

They did every together since their connection in elementary school. It was a cool friendship; each one of them would give a five-star rating.

Christine told the others that she didn't believe in ghosts, no matter what people said or experienced.

Dan and Oliver were on the fence as to whether ghosts were real or not. It was Joan who was the staunch believer. She said she saw ghosts as a child. They all laughed around her ideas, poking fun at her in a delightful way.

Dan suggested they all see the so-called haunted house at the edge of town. They hopped into their car and drove on over.

The house itself wasn't much to look at, thought Christine, making jokes about how it didn't even look "haunted." It looked normal. They all made funny comments about it, as was their fashion.

"It that a rumbling I hear?" Amy asked her friend Josh.

"Yeah," said Josh, "Some say that's the sound of the explosion that took place that day when the house exploded six years ago."

"Really? That's kind of spooky."

"You think that's spooky, wait a few minutes, and you'll hear what sounds like screams."

Sure enough, the sounds of screams carried in the wind swirled around them.

"Let's get out of here," Amy added.

"Yeah," Josh said, turning away from the charred ruins of a burnt-out house. "It's kind of sad, six years ago four high-school kids who called themselves the Musketeers went the house. They just opened the door, and a gas leak explosion killed all of them."

"Oh my God, that must've been horrible!" Amy added, "It's haunted, alright!"

XXXIX

The aliens were smart enough to quarantine every intelligent species they collected. They knew the workings of bacteria and viruses common to many different life forms on distant planets.

When one of their ships came to the Earth eons ago, they discovered and an "ape-like" creature. They brought several of the beings on board to investigate the possibility of intelligent life.

Several of the apes, to the surprise of the aliens, awoke from their induced anesthesia, breaking quarantine. They broke free from their bonds and attacked several of the aliens.

The aliens released the remaining apes, concluding that they were just too savage for intelligence.

The apes that attacked the aliens, however, were infected with microbes, viruses, and DNA from the alien blood,

Those apes slowly began to change and develop in unexpected ways, spreading their increased molecular structure and intelligence throughout their species.

Other ships came back to the planet, and they came to realize that they had infected the Earthers, but they were still far too naturally savage for them.

Ever since then, they've been watching Earthers from afar, maintaining a safe distance, but monitoring them to see how far the infectious evolutionary process will take shape. Will Earthers become highly self-sufficient and intelligent creatures or remain the savages they were recognized to be and wipe themselves out?

XL

The chief of the Ingundi tribe knew his younger brother was planning the death of the shaman's oldest son, for the reading the scribe gave him about being victorious in battle was far from the truth.

He could hear his brother talking to himself after drinking too much ale. The battle cost him his oldest son, and he wanted revenge. It burned him like red-hot coals on a bed of dried leaves.

He wanted the shaman to feel his grief, his loss.

The chief did not know how to handle the affair. If word got out that the tribal leader knew and the shaman's son's body found dead, it would mean the end of his reign.

While his brother was sitting drunk, the chief took a ritual knife to threaten him and force him to forget such foolishness. The brother jumped up, grabbing the knife from him, and told him don't ever try to stop him.

He would keep his older brother's knife and use it to slay the shaman's son. The village people might think their chief did the deed.

The night that he planned to commit the crime, he waited in the bushes in the forest. In the shadows, he saw a figure of a boy; he jumped out and stabbed him repeatedly, only to learn it was his youngest son. The shaman's son was ill; the shaman asked the young boy to deliver some herbs to the village.

At the murder of his youngest son, the spirit of his oldest son returned and took revenge against his father.

The villagers found their bodies. An oracle reading told the shaman to drug his oldest and made him ill the night before.

The chief only said that someone stole his knife; he didn't know it was his brother.

XLI

The prisoners marched wearily, leaving Marshall to look back over his shoulders to see how many more like him were behind him. The line seemed to fade in the dust swirling near the horizon. So many, he thought.

A painful electrical charge surged through his ankle bracelet as the cackle from an alien soldier reminded him to look forward.

How did so many of us get captured? He couldn't believe it.

He felt the defeat he saw. Marshall was broken.

The scientist monitoring him in the lab were thrilled that the sprayed mist they released in the control room had the effect they anticipated.

They applauded themselves, expecting a similar response from the military. The scientists looked forward to an increase in their annual budget.

They worked feverishly over the last six months on a spray-mist from alien blood. Looking to use against the very same aliens they were fighting on the planet Zeros. The aliens didn't possess the technology to reach Earth. Earthers wanted another world to conquer for its resources.

When Marshall and a few other test-subjects came out of the control room, the scientists gathered to interview them on the hallucinatory effects of the mist.

Marshall couldn't believe he was still on Earth with other men from his unit who volunteered for the procedure. The mist made it seem he was back on Zeros.

Before the scientists and doctors started asking questions, Marshall and the others suddenly began turning into ferocious creatures, slaying many of the scientists outside the control room. Marshall, or what was left of him, sprayed other researchers with his breath, changing them into beasts like him.

The carnage spread throughout the military base and headed for a major city. The aliens from Zeros had arrived after all!

XLII

It was just a coin, or at least that's what most people thought. It and a few others like it were old, and no one officially knew the currency or part of the world from whence it came.

Stories grew about the battlefields, the sunken vessels where it laid deep in the ocean, and the other exotic places and times throughout history where people found it.

The coin was found, lost, then found again throughout the centuries.

After being lost for decades, William James, a surveyor working at an ancient site, discovered it stuck beneath an old pillar.

It looked old, it looked pretty, and it looked unusual. After scrutinizing it in the sunlight, William decided it was a lucky find and placed it in his pocket.

In a flash, he found himself transported hundreds of years in the future, aboard a space frigate heading back to Earth with rare ore samples.

Crew members were rushing back and forth across the deck as smoke was billowing out all over.

"Are you just going to stand there, or are you going to help?" a shipmate screamed at him. "We're about to crash!"

Sure enough, when he looked out a portal, the Earth appeared as he had never seen it, and they were headed for it.

William was in a state of shock; he didn't know where to go or what to do. He didn't even know how he got there in the first place.

Within minutes the ship was lost, the entire crew along with William James.

In amongst the charred rubble was a shiny coin, waiting to be found.

XLIII

Everyone knew where the ogre lived, or at least they thought they knew, saying that it was near a river-crossing, under the stone bridge to the south. They were wrong. It wasn't so much as where it lived as to where it roamed.

It seemed to have an appetite for small children, boys, girls; it didn't matter.

Townspeople on both sides of the river were alarmed. They tried tracking the ogre, but it alluded them every time.

A robust and burly woodsman appeared in one of the villages, known for his hunting prowess. He stood with his ax and waited for the village elders to speak to him.

"Let's get straight to the point," he barked, "What will you give me if I kill that beast of an ogre and bring you his head on a pike?" He looked hard at the elders waiting for a response.

They consulted amongst themselves and said, "The most we can offer you is three gold coins, for we are poor."

"The village across the river offered me four gold pieces," he lied.

Again, the elders talked amongst themselves that that ogre's head on a pike would speak well of their village.

"We are willing to offer you five gold pieces."

The woodsman grabbed his ax, "Fine, that will do." He went off to slay the ogre.

He already knew the ogre's trail, so he patiently waited in the dark woods, jumping the ogre as it passed. It was a violent fight; the ogre bit his leg, growling, "I now become you!" That's when the woodsman chopped off its head.

He brought the head to the town on a pike. They paid him, and when the gold touched his hand, he changed into an ogre, devouring three elder's heads before escaping into the forest.

XLIV

She had trouble reading The Book of Incantations; there was some uncommonly wrong with it. She never realized that the book had a curse on it and that anyone in her family bloodline would never be able to use it.

Her father had betrayed the mage who owned the book by pushing him in an iron maiden and sealing it shut. As the sharp spikes entered the mage's body, the mage cursed her grandfather and his bloodline.

Her father shared the same lie; his father told him that the book was a gift for the loyalty of his grandfather.

She never truly questioned her father's disappearance, why he left home, never to return, or even consider the circumstances surrounding the departure of her grandfather. Did they both go mad trying to figure out the conjuring in the book and decided to give up and leave?

Men! They were weak; it was her belief. She, however, wouldn't give up the way they did, but what she didn't know was that every day, the words in the spell-book rearranged themselves to be useless to her.

She knew something was a mist. She decided to memorize one spell and one spell one only, instead of trying several incantations.

Again, she never realized that as the words change in the book, they also turned in her memory. Finally, the chant worded itself to bring about a disappearance spell. What she came to believe as a spell for making her visible again did not exist.

When she tried it, like her father and her grandfather before her, she vanished to another dimension, never to return.

XLV

Ming and her younger brother Mao were riding the train with their grandmother. The locomotive was still new in China, and only members of wealthy families could afford to ride them.

Fortunately for them, their father was a minister to the royal family, and he and their mother wanted them brought to the palace grounds to be with them.

It was an enjoyable ride. Even Ming's grandmother was enjoying the view and sites; after she was able to tolerate the smoke from the engine.

High above the clouds, five dragons circled the giant worm they saw below them. They had never seen the like. Their matriarch decided to feast on the creature below.

All of them flew downward with remarkable speed.

Ming's brother pointed to the shadows on the ground, which looked like enormous flying wings. Everyone on the train started screaming as the train was attacked and lifted into the air,

The dragons breathed fire on their prey, and they roared with a passion for capturing their meal. The people shrieked wildly, some falling to their death as the dragons rose higher and higher, carrying their prey to their mountain range.

Ming's parents waited at the station for a train that would never arrive.

XLVI

It was as if she was in a dream. She was in a strange land with vines shooting out from all over her body. Somewhere in the distance, there was sunlight, or at least she thought it looked like the sun.

Animals seemed to be moving all around her. Deer would come to her and rub against her legs. Squirrels took fancy to running up to her eyelids and opening them up occasionally.

There was a voice, far away, that echoed, "Scalpel." She thought that was funny. Who would be in the woods saying that?

Her favorite song was quietly playing somewhere in the background.

Suddenly she sprouted wings and began flying above the trees.

She awoke by the tap of someone's hand on a microphone, "Dr. Feldstein, Dr. Feldstein? Can you hear me? Can you hear me?"

There was a pause, "Andrew, make sure the cables are connected."

"They are," Andrew responded.

"Dr. Feldstein?"

She couldn't open her eyes, saying, "I can't see, I can't see!"

"Margaret, turn on the video cam. I told you to have it on before."

After a click, she could see everyone and what appeared to be her body on a medical table.

"Where am I?" she asked.

"Wow, I didn't think it was possible, but we moved your brain out of your dying body and made it part of the central computer system as you requested."

The statement shocked her senses. The experience was not what she expected. There was an enduring silence that would exist for years to come as she provided the space colony with a running electrical system. She just never spoke again; Dr. Feldstein's brain did what it had to do, but she preferred to dream.

XLVII

The crew of the Nautilus PX-29 was returning from another deep-space mission. They knew that their time in space and time for Earthlings would be different. The explorers were hard-wired for deep space travel.

Five years passed since their last return. They didn't know what they would find on their homeworld. The music, the fashion, the social way of life was probably a lot different from when they left.

When they entered the solar system, there was no communication from any of the outer planetary space stations.

The Nautilus crew was surprised by the lack of any kind of official acknowledgment of their return. The closer they got to their planet, the more concerned they grew.

When they flew passed Mars, they met three heavily armed cruisers. A species called Korileans. The crew stunned and confused by the sight of these massage ships. Theirs was not a war vessel.

Using their universal translator. The captain opened communication with what appeared to be the lead ship. Wishing to speak to one in command. Claiming that his crew didn't want a fight; they were only returning home.

The ship's screen displayed an unusually vicious creature, who surprised them by speaking English without a translator.

"Your planet Earth is now Colony 256 of the Korilean empire. Thank you for the craft, Voyager, it taught us many things about your world, and it guided us here. We conquered your pathetic planet two solar cycles ago. Now, do you wish to surrender your vessel or die like so many of your kind?"

The Nautilus captain looked at the helmsman and asked, "How quick can we make light speed?"

"Not quick enough!" the Korilean captain answered, surmising the Earth captain's intentions, destroying the Nautilus.

XLVIII

As Helen rose to her feet after falling, she noticed that the sunlight shining a moment ago was now a gray mist. She looked around while pulling herself up. She could see through the fog a figure slowly coming toward her.

Fear traveled up her spine. She couldn't make out the shadowy figure. She was about to run away from it when finally, she saw the face of a kind, aged woman.

"Oh, I see another one has fallen through the door," the old woman chuckled softly.

"What? Where am I? What is this place?" Helen blubbered.

"Oh, I'm sorry, my child. You must've fallen through one of the doors."

"Doors? What are you talking about?" Helen stammered.

"Why, one of the many doors of conscious worlds. Portals that open and close like clockwork all over the universe. I am a shepherd, and I can guide you back to your world."

"Really?" Helen sounded agitated, "What are those flashing lights?"

"Those are doors, here let me take you to your door."

"I don't need your help; I just want to get the hell out of here," Helen shouted, she was too impatient as she started running for the nearest flash.

"No, wait," the shepherd told her, "I that's not your portal, it could —"

Helen disappeared before the shepherd finished. "— take you another time or another world."

The shepherd stopped and shook, for she knew that portal all too well; it leads to a place called Hell.

"Why the hideous mask?" Swift Hawk asked the Healer who came out of the forest in the morning light.

"I could ask the same thing about you," the Healer replied.

"What do you mean by that?"

"Oh, it's visible for anyone to see. You've been wearing one since Dancing Flower left the village three moons ago."

Swift Hawk walked up to the Healer, saying, "The truth is I cared for Dancing Flower and did not want her to leave us."

"Again, you put on another mask."

He saw the surprised look on Swift Hawk's fast, but continued, "Is it not because you gave Dancing Flower the power stone I entrusted in your care? You're unable to face me as the man you were, so you go around your fellow tribal brothers and sisters, hoping no one would know your crime."

"Crime? What crime? I just gave her a power stone, that's all," Swift Hawk asserted.

"A power stone, she and anyone, but you were forbidden to touch!" accused the Healer. "They found her ashes and her neck bracelet on the road to our sister village some days ago."

What? No!" cried Swift Hawk.

"Here, now take this mask," insisted the Healer.

"No, I'd rather not," Swift Hawk complained.

"I said to take the mask and show it to the lake," Healer ordered, forcing it into Swift Hawk's hands.

Swift Hawk's heart was troubled as he walked to the lake. He knew he never honestly believed in power stones. Giving Dancing Flower the power stone was just a joke; he meant no harm.

When he reached the lake, he bent over to show the hideous mask to the waters, only to scream at the sight of seeing that his face and the mask looked one and the same.

L

The wormhole appeared stable enough for them to send probes into and investigate. Decades of searching for a stable wormhole passed before the discovery of Newton's Way.

The walls of the wormhole remained steady. The probes, however, didn't send much enough information back to the science vessel as to what was on the other side.

Science Officer, John Metcalf, prepared his crew to be the first ship to investigate the anomaly.

Newton's Way, discovered by his mother's great, great, great grandfather, and John grew up, mesmerized with the hope of one day traveling through the find.

Sending out two probes ahead of him, John prepared to enter, leaving a small fleet of ships behind to receive his readings.

The voyage was going well when halfway through the wormhole, the probes stopped, and his ship flew right by them.

The crew spotted many other probes from other vessels, some alien, still curious, they continued,

Members of his crew could not explain the phenomena or the other alien probes.

Suddenly the opening at the other end appeared, and the crew realized they were the first humans to transverse a stable wormhole.

They cheered and bought out bottles of champagne to celebrate, only to have their craft swallowed by a colossal worm-like, space creature as they cleared the other side.

As the beast crunched hard on his ship, John realized the wormhole was only a lure to catch space vessels. His spacecraft was nothing more than a fish on a hook.

Story/Word Count
(For those of you interested in such things.)

Story	Word Count	Story	Word Count
I	297	XXVI	214
II	247	XXVII	300
III	300	XXVIII	222
IV	296	XXIX	245
V	249	XXX	229
VI	299	XXXI	287
VII	300	XXXII	267
VIII	286	XXXIII	300
IX	300	XXXIV	274
X	236	XXXV	299
XI	276	XXXVI	257
XII	300	XXXVII	248
XIII	254	XXXVIII	300
XIV	254	XXXIX	220
XV	213	XL	299
XVI	292	XLI	294
XVII	296	XLII	269
XVIII	300	XLIII	300
XIX	297	XLIV	270
XX	285	XLV	205
XXI	300	XLVI	286
XXII	294	XLVII	288
XXIII	273	XLVIII	248
XXIV	286	XLIX	297
XXV	297	L	248

About the Author

Amurá Oñaā came into this world pretty much like the rest of us.
A lover of music - a musician, art - an artist/sculptor,
and literature - a poet/lyricist/writer, still finding his way
through this maze called life.